BIONICLE™

Mystery of
Metru Nui

BIONICLE™

FIND THE POWER,
LIVE THE LEGEND

The legend comes alive in these exciting BIONICLE™ books:

BIONICLE™ Chronicles

#1 Tale of the Toa
#2 Beware the Bohrok
#3 Makuta's Revenge
#4 Tales of the Masks

The Official Guide to BIONICLE™

BIONICLE™ Collector's Sticker Book

BIONICLE™: Mask of Light

BIONICLE™

Mystery of Metru Nui

by Greg Farshtey

SCHOLASTIC INC.
New York Toronto London Auckland Sydney
Mexico City New Delhi Hong Kong Buenos Aires

For Evan, who shows the world every day what
being a hero really means, from his best pal.
— GF

ISBN 0-439-60731-0

12 11 10 9 8 7 6 5 4 3 2   3 4 5 6 7 8/0

Printed in the U.S.A.
First printing, February 2004

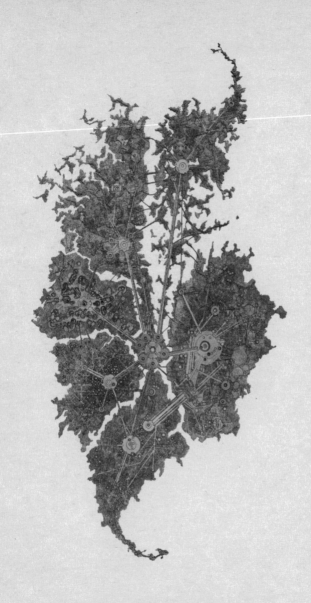

The City of Metru Nui

INTRODUCTION

Turaga Vakama, elder of the Mata Nui village of fire, stood on a high cliff overlooking the beach. Far below, Matoran from all over the island were hard at work constructing boats for the long journey back home.

Vakama shook his head. Home. It had been so long since any of them had seen it, and the Matoran did not even remember living anywhere but Mata Nui. Only the six village elders recalled when and why they first came to the island, and for thousands of years, they had locked that secret away inside themselves.

The Turaga turned at the sound of another's approach. It was Tahu Nuva, Toa of Fire and leader of the heroes of Mata Nui. "How go the labors, Turaga?" he asked.

"Quite well, Toa Tahu. We will soon have enough boats to carry us all back to the island city of Metru Nui. The Po-Matoran are at work widening the tunnels so we can carry the boats to the subterranean sea."

Tahu nodded as his mind flashed back to the events of the past months. After the final confrontation with Makuta, master of shadows, the Toa had discovered a new island far beneath the surface of Mata Nui. It sat in the center of a silver sea of protodermis, and they could see few details of it from the shore. But Vakama insisted that this place was Metru Nui, the original home of the Matoran, to which they must return.

Even more startling, the Turaga revealed that Metru Nui had once been home to six other Toa, heroes who existed long before Tahu and the others ever appeared. But Vakama had said nothing about the fate of those early "Toa Metru," or whether they might still be waiting on Metru Nui.

"I have been in council with the other Toa,"

said Tahu. "I have come to ask you to tell us all about this new land, Metru Nui. If we are going to journey there and protect the Matoran from any threats that might lurk in that place, we must know everything."

Vakama turned and walked away from the cliff. "Indeed you must. But I will warn you, Tahu: The tales of Metru Nui are tales of sacrifice, betrayal, great danger, and yes, heroes as well. Their telling may change much of what you think you know about myself, the other Turaga, and the Matoran you have served all this time."

"I — we — are prepared for that, Turaga," replied Tahu. "The Toa have gathered at the Great Temple of Kini-Nui. They wait only for you."

"Then let them wait no longer, Tahu."

The seven Toa — Tahu, Kopaka, Gali, Pohatu, Onua, Lewa, and Takanuva — stood silently around the Amaja Circle. The Turaga had used that sandpit and the stones within it many times to tell tales of the past and future.

The Turaga of Fire placed the stone representing Mata Nui in the center of the circle and began. "In the time before time, long before any Matoran set foot on the island of Mata Nui, there was a city of legends. Hear now the first tale of Metru Nui. . . ."

Kapura walked slowly along the outskirts of the district of Ta-Metru, his eyes scanning the ground. Most of the homes and factories in this part of the metru had been abandoned lately, with the residents moving closer to the heart of the district. It was Kapura's job to make sure nothing of importance had been left behind.

He paused in front of a massive, blackened building that had once housed a forge. Here, construction tools and other equipment had been cast from molten protodermis before being sent on to Po-Metru for finishing. Now, in the interest of safety, that work had been transferred away from the outskirts by order of the city's elder, Turaga Dume. Kapura spotted a staff used in the sport of kolhii on the ground and bent down to pick it up, only to discover the handle was cracked.

He walked on. This was an important task, his fellow workers had told him, and important tasks were best done slowly and carefully.

Had Kapura looked up, he would have seen the skyline of Ta-Metru, "home of the makers." Cone-shaped factories, scorched by ages of use, stood next to the homes of smiths and crafters. These were the Matoran who molded protodermis, the substance of which everything on Metru Nui was made, into thousands of shapes and forms. A molten river of raw protodermis ran through the center of the district, drawn from below the city and fed into the Great Furnace. From there, it traveled to each factory to be turned into masks, tools, and anything else that might be needed.

Dominating the skyline was the Coliseum, home to Turaga Dume and the tallest building in all of Metru Nui. For as long as anyone could remember, the sight of the Coliseum had brought a feeling of safety and security to Matoran. But now . . .

Kapura counted slowly as he walked. Six, seven, eight — at least eight of the workers at his factory had vanished lately. Where they disappeared to, and why, no one knew. But there were plenty of rumors.

The Matoran stopped. Something had moved off to the right. It didn't sound like another Matoran, or even a wild Rahi beast. It was a soft, slithering sound, as if something was dragging itself across the ground. The sound grew louder and seemed to multiply. Kapura felt the urge to run, but his feet would not move.

He forced himself to turn around and look. Four thick, blackened, twisted vines were snaking their way out of cracks in the ground, weaving in the air as if momentarily unsure of what to do. Then they wrapped themselves around the empty factory and began to climb, winding around again and again until they covered the building from top to bottom.

Kapura's eyes widened as the vines started to squeeze. Solid protodermis crumbled before their strength. The building groaned and cracked, collapsing in on itself in a matter of seconds. As if satisfied, the vines pulled away and began to move toward another structure.

It was then that Kapura found his voice. But he could speak only one word, and that in a horrified whisper:

"Morbuzakh."

In another section of the city, a second Matoran was also thinking about the dreaded Morbuzakh plant. The vines had been appearing on the outskirts of the city for some time, wrecking structures and forcing residents to flee. No one knew where they came from or how to stop them. All that was known was that everyone who challenged the Morbuzakh vanished, never to be seen again.

But this particular Matoran wasn't worried about the damage the plant was causing. Instead, all his attention was focused on a tablet decorated with a most interesting carving. The picture showed the combined power of six disks defeating a gigantic Morbuzakh root. Disks — called

Kanoka in the Matoran language — were a common sight in Metru Nui. The spheres were created in every metru and used primarily for sport, as well as for defense against the wild beasts called Rahi. Disks found to be of the right purity and power level were forged into Masks of Power. But the disks in the carving could not simply be any old Kanoka, the Matoran knew. These had to be the six Great Disks of legend.

Under the picture of each Great Disk was inscribed the section of the city where it could be found and the name of a Matoran: Nuhrii, Ahkmou, Vhisola, Tehutti, Ehrye, and Orkahm.

When he was done examining the carving, the Matoran turned to Nidhiki, the strange, four-legged being who had brought it. "What is it I'm supposed to do?"

"I would think it would be obvious," hissed Nidhiki from the shadows. "Get the six Great Disks. I don't care how. Then give them to me and I will take them somewhere . . . safe."

The Matoran frowned. "If they truly exist, these are the six most powerful Kanoka disks in

Metru Nui. They would be beyond price. What do I get out of this?"

"You will be well paid, Matoran," Nidhiki replied, smiling in a particularly nasty way. "Plus you get one more benefit, if you're successful: I won't come looking for you."

"All right, all right. I get the idea. But why is this so important? Even if these Matoran could get their hands on the Great Disks, they wouldn't dare try to stop the Morbuzakh themselves."

"It's not Matoran we're worried about," came the answer. "It's so-called heroes — Toa Metru. Six Toa Metru."

With that, Nidhiki was gone. The Matoran watched him go, thinking, *Six Toa Metru? How is that possible?*

Moments before, they had been Matoran. Six strangers, each from a different metru, brought together by a plea for help from Toa Lhikan, the hero of Metru Nui. Now, in the heart of the Great Temple in Ga-Metru, they had been transformed. Where once six Matoran had stood, there now existed six new Toa Metru.

Whenua, once an archivist in Onu-Metru and now the Toa of Earth, voiced the thoughts of them all. "Since when are Matoran just zapped into Toa?"

Nuju, former seer and now Toa of Ice, answered, "When uncertain times lie ahead."

Vakama, Ta-Metru's most skilled mask maker and the new Toa of Fire, looked down at his new form. It was hard to believe that this new power had been granted to him. He remembered the city's protector, Toa Lhikan, giving him a powerful artifact called a Toa stone and a map to a spot in the Great Temple. Then Lhikan was captured by two strange creatures, one a four-legged foe and the other huge and powerful. Heeding his last wish, Vakama had taken the Toa stone to the temple, only to run into five other Matoran with similar missions.

They placed their stones on top of the shrine dedicated to Toa. Before their eyes, the

Toa stones began to pulsate and then rose into the air. Beams of elemental energy shot from them, bathing the Matoran in light, changing them, granting them power. When it was over, the Matoran had become Toa Metru, destined guardians of Metru Nui.

But are we ready for this? Am I? Vakama asked himself. He didn't have an answer.

The other Toa had begun selecting their tools from a compartment inside the suva shrine. Vakama looked over what remained and chose a powerful Kanoka disk launcher. It was a larger version of what he had used in the past to play the sport of kolhii. The familiarity of it made him feel a little more comfortable in his new body.

Matau, Toa of Air, chuckled. "Nice choice — for playing Matoran games, mask maker."

"Hey, look at this," Onewa, the new Toa Metru of Stone, said. He reached into the tool compartment and emerged with six Kanoka disks. Each was a different color, and each bore the likeness of a Mask of Power. But what drew the attention of the new heroes was that the masks matched the ones they now wore.

"What does it mean?" asked Nokama, Toa Metru of Water.

"Perhaps that we were not chosen at random for this?" Vakama suggested. "Perhaps this is our destiny."

"What did Toa Lhikan say we could expect, Vakama? What are we meant to do now that we are Toa?" asked Whenua. Nokama and Onewa drew in closer, anxious to hear the answer as well.

"He said —" Vakama began.

Then, suddenly, his mind was somewhere else. He could see day being consumed by night, Metru Nui collapsing into ruin, then miraculously restored. Six Kanoka disks flew at him from out of the darkness, forcing him to duck and dodge. They shot past him, then hovered in the air and unleashed their power on the Morbuzakh plant. Before their energies, the plant withered and died. Their task done, the Great Disks merged together to form a single one of immense power, and . . .

Then the vision was gone. But the chill inside Vakama told him it had not just been an idle daydream. "Metru Nui was destroyed. I saw it! Six Great Kanoka Disks were headed right for me, and . . ."

"Thanks for dream-sharing," Matau said, shaking his head.

"No, we must find them. They can defeat the Morbuzakh and free the city from danger. That would prove we are worthy to be Toa Metru!" Vakama continued.

The others looked at him, some doubtful, some evidently willing to believe. They had all heard the tales of the Great Disks before. It was said they contained enormous power, but the only clue to their location was that one was hidden in each metru. If the disks were used by someone with good intent, they could change the world for the better. If their user was evil, Metru Nui and all its inhabitants might be erased forever.

"Then find them we shall," said Nokama. "I saw a carving in the temple that might help us.

Something about finding the Great Disks by seeking the unfamiliar within the familiar. But the rest seemed to be . . . riddles. What do you think, Vakama?"

But the Toa of Fire was not listening. In his mind's eye, he saw six Matoran, each with a Great Disk. He knew their names but could not see their faces. Worse, the shadows behind them were alive with danger. Vakama could see a pair of fierce red eyes hovering in the darkness and a four-legged creature stalking the Matoran. He had seen that figure before, in real life, struggling with Toa Lhikan. Vakama knew how powerful and evil this being was, and the memory made him shudder.

"Nuhrii . . . Orkahm . . . Vhisola . . . Ahk-mou . . . Ehrye . . . Tehutti," Vakama muttered. "They can decipher the riddles. They can help us find the Great Disks. But beware of a dark hunter who walks on four legs."

"You have spent too much time at the forge, fire-spitter," answered Onewa. "Your head needs cooling down."

"I trust Vakama," Nokama said. "If he believes those six Matoran can help us find the disks, then we must seek them out. When we have found them, we will meet back here. Good luck to us all."

If my vision is true, thought Vakama, *we will need far, far more than luck.*

The Toa Metru said their farewells and went their separate ways. Only Nokama and Vakama remained behind, staring up at the Great Temple.

"Vakama, do you really think Metru Nui is in danger? Perhaps from something more frightening than the Morbuzakh?"

"I know there is darkness coming," Vakama replied. "Toa Lhikan said we had to stop it. He said we had to save the 'heart of the city.' I don't know how or why, but we have been chosen."

"Then may the Great Beings protect us all," said the Toa of Water.

Toa Nokama turned and began walking farther into Ga-Metru. All was quiet. This was traditionally the most peaceful section of Metru Nui, home to scholars and scientists. Often the only sound that could be heard was the rush of the protodermis falls.

Ga-Matoran passed her on the street, looking up with awe and wonder. Some were old friends, but no one seemed to recognize her. When she did stop someone and say hello, the Matoran shied away from her and scurried off.

Nokama frowned. She had never nursed any dreams of becoming a Toa. She enjoyed her life as a teacher in Ga-Metru, gaining new wisdom each day and passing it on to others. Her happiest moments had been spent in a classroom or showing her students the ancient carvings at the protodermis fountains. Now that she was a "hero," she was starting to realize what a lonely role it could be.

At least my very first task will not be a hard one, she thought. *Vhisola will gladly help me.*

As she walked along the canals past the beautiful temples of Ga-Metru, she remembered when she had first met her friend. Vhisola had been a student in one of Nokama's classes. The Ga-Matoran had been eager to learn, almost too eager. In her enthusiasm, she always seemed to make some mistake or other. Then she would get flustered and make another and another, until her project was a mess.

Eventually, Nokama realized that if she spent extra time with Vhisola, the Matoran did better work. They became friends and still were, even if sometimes it was a stormy friendship. The more time they spent together, the more time Vhisola wanted to spend. If Nokama said she was too busy to practice kolhii or explore the canals that day, Vhisola would sulk.

Their last argument had been a bad one, but Nokama was certain they had patched things up. Certainly Vhisola would not hesitate to help if she knew the fate of the city depended upon it.

Nokama rapped on the door of Vhisola's small home. No one answered. When she rapped again, one of the neighbors emerged and said, "Who are you?"

"I'm —" Nokama began, then hesitated. If she gave her name, she would probably have to give a long explanation of why she was no longer a Matoran. Instead, she replied, "I'm the Toa of Water. Have you seen Vhisola?"

"A Toa? Here?" said the Ga-Matoran excitedly. "I know of Toa Lhikan, of course, but I have never met a Toa up close. Where did you come from? Are you here to stay?"

"Please, just answer my question. Have you seen Vhisola today?"

The Ga-Matoran shook her head. "No, not lately. Is she in some trouble?"

"I hope not," Nokama said. She tried the door, but it was locked. Still, she was now a Toa, and much stronger than before. A little bit of force and the door flew open.

Although they had known each other a long time, Nokama had never been inside Vhisola's home. Now she saw why. Every inch of the walls was covered with carvings of Nokama, records of her achievements, copies of awards she had won. There was nothing in the room to say that Vhisola even lived there.

Once the shock had passed, Nokama began to look around for any sign of where Vhisola might have gone. Her eye was caught by lights flashing on a table. Coming closer, she saw that the lights were part of a map of Ga-Metru. Certain sections lit up, flashed for an instant, then went dark again. With no better idea, Nokama moved her hand from section to section as they lit, hoping to find a pattern.

There was a sound of stone grinding against stone. Then the center of the map opened up and a tablet rose from inside the table. Nokama picked it up and saw it was Vhisola's journal. She almost put it back — then she remembered the real fear in Vakama's face when he spoke of his visions. If Metru Nui was in danger, Nokama could not afford to ignore any possible clue.

She scanned the last few entries and found nothing of note. But the last left her numb with fear. It read: "At first, I couldn't believe it when I heard Nokama was a Toa. Now that she is a hero, she will never have any time for me. I've spent so much time practicing my kolhii and trying to do better schoolwork, all to impress her ... and now she will just want to spend time with her new Toa friends. Well, I'll show her. Once I get my hands on that Great Disk, I'll be the one people have to look up to. She will be the one they ignore!"

She knows I am a Toa? How ... ? Oh, Vhisola, Nokama said to herself, *I never meant to ignore you. You don't know the danger you could be in.*

There was no time for worry or regret. There were only two other places Vhisola spent time at, the school and the kolhii practice field. There was no practice scheduled for today, so maybe she was in class. If she wasn't, it might already be too late.

Nokama turned to leave, then stopped. Out the window, she could see the familiar, spiderlike shapes of Vahki moving down the avenue. They enforced the law and kept order in Metru Nui, but even so, the sight of them had always filled Nokama with an unnamed dread. Vhisola's neighbor was talking to the squad leader.

Maybe she sent for them, Nokama thought. *Maybe she doesn't believe I am a Toa — especially since I can hardly believe it myself.*

The Vahki would want to bring her to Turaga Dume for questioning, and there was no time for that. She would have to get away from them.

Outside the house, the Ga-Matoran neighbor was doing her best to make the Vahki understand. "She said she was a Toa. Well, how do I know that's what she is? Maybe it's some trick of the Morbuzakh. Anyway, I know my duty, so I sent for you."

The Vahki nodded and signaled to the others in its squad to surround the house. Once certain that its stun staff was fully charged, it headed for Vhisola's home.

Nokama chose that moment to burst out of the door. Before the Vahki could react, she rushed past him and dove into the protodermis canal. Extending her hydro blades in front of her, she knifed through the liquid. The Vahki wasted no time in pursuing, taking to the sky to follow her course.

No Matoran could hope to outdistance a Vahki, but a Toa was another matter. Her Toa tools gave her an edge in speed, though she knew it would not be enough. She would have to rely on her most powerful advantage — her knowledge of Ga-Metru.

Up ahead, the canal continued toward the Great Temple, but there was a narrow branch to the left that fed protodermis into a central reservoir. Nokama glanced over her shoulder. The Vahki were temporarily out of sight. She whipped around the corner and down the feeder branch, plunging into the reservoir far below.

Nokama dove deep into the cool protodermis, then kicked hard and broke the surface. The reservoir was a huge, circular chamber, lit by lightstones embedded in the ceiling. Every sound echoed and re-echoed in the chamber, from the lapping of the waves to Nokama's breathing. But the one sound she did not hear was Vahki up above.

Satisfied that they had given up, Nokama dove down to the bottom of the tank and swam into another feeder branch. *The other Toa have probably already found their Matoran,* she thought. *How they will laugh when they hear of the difficulty I had!*

Vhisola's classes were held in one of the many ornate domes that dotted Ga-Metru. Her instructor was little help but did suggest that perhaps the Matoran had closeted herself in the lab to finish some overdue work.

It was only a short walk to the lab, but for some reason Nokama felt she had to run. The sight of the door blown off its hinges told her she was already too late.

The inside of the lab looked worse. Furniture was overturned, tablets scattered and smashed as if a windstorm had torn through the place. A lab worker was doing his best to straighten up when Nokama entered.

"What happened here?"

The Matoran jumped. "Don't do that! You startled me! I thought that . . . thing had come back here again."

"I'm sorry," Nokama said, realizing that her new appearance probably was a bit intimidating. "What 'thing' are you talking about?"

"I don't know. Four legs, some kind of claw tool — ripped the place apart. He stole all of Vhisola's research notes, all except one." The Matoran pointed to a shattered tablet on the ground.

Nokama knelt down and began sifting through the fragments, matching the carvings on them together like a puzzle. When she was done, there was an image of a huge Morbuzakh root and six Great Disks bringing it down. Beneath each disk was written the metru it came from and a three-digit code.

Vakama was right! There is a connection between the Great Disks and the Morbuzakh. But why would anyone want to stop us from ending that threat?

Then she caught sight of something else, half hidden by an overturned bench. It was a map of the Le-Metru chute system, stamped with the name Orkahm. *What would this be doing here?* Nokama wondered.

She looked up at the lab worker, who was watching her intently. "The rest of her notes — have you seen them?"

"Hey, I just take care of the lab. I never —"

Nokama rose to her full height. Looking down on the Matoran, she repeated slowly, "Have you seen them?"

The Matoran's gaze dropped to the floor. "All right. She showed them to me once. Said something about a Great Disk making her somebody. Her notes were all about the Morbuzakh, but they didn't make any sense to me. She made copies of everything and said she was taking them home."

"For the sake of Ga-Metru and the whole city, I hope they are still there," said Nokama.

She returned to Vhisola's home through the canals. As she feared, there was still a Vahki patrolling the area. Reasoning with it would be a waste of time. Vahki didn't listen. They were trained to see movement and to react. She needed a distraction.

Well, I am supposed to be the Toa of Water, she said to herself. *Let us see if that is only a name.*

It was the hardest thing Nokama had ever attempted. Extending her twin tools, she strained to draw moisture from the air. At one point, she thought sure she would black out and drift away on the canal. But finally, she could feel one of the most powerful of elements coming under her control.

Two narrow streams of water were all she could manage at first, but they were enough. She targeted a bit of ornamentation on a house down the avenue. The water struck it head-on, knocking it from its perch with a resounding crash. The Vahki paused, turned, and moved off to investigate.

Nokama bolted for the house. Inside, she searched frantically for any possible hiding place. The four-legged creature had obviously not been here, unless he had suddenly grown neater. But where had Vhisola hidden the notes? What would be the one place that would be special to her?

Then her eyes settled on the largest picture of herself. Nokama almost dreaded being proven right, but she was — behind the picture was a safe with three dials. There was no time to try to guess the combination. It had to be one of the codes that had been on the tablet, or her search would end in failure.

At first, she considered using the Ga-Metru code, but that almost seemed too obvious. She tried the Ta-Metru code, the Onu-Metru code, the Po-Metru code, and the others, all to no end. But when she spun the dial to the three digits of the Ga-Metru code, the door swung open. Inside was a pile of tablets, all with Vhisola's distinctive carvings on them. Nokama glanced at each one until she found the crucial piece of information.

It was a carving of the Great Temple with a powerful disk pictured beside it. It had been there all the time!

Vhisola must have gone there to retrieve the Great Disk, thought Nokama. *But if she doesn't know about that four-legged monster . . .*

Nokama turned and raced out of the house. She didn't even worry that the Vahki might pursue her again. *Let it follow me! I could use the help!*

As she sped through the canals heading for the Great Temple, Nokama remembered one of her first conversations with Vhisola. "Everyone has a special talent," she had told the Matoran. "You simply have to discover the one that is yours." Now that she knew Vhisola's plan had been to take the Great Disk for herself and use it for personal gain, she wondered if the Matoran's "special talent" was deception.

She emerged from the canals near the temple but was stopped short by the sight of a crowd of Matoran some distance away. They were craning their necks to look up at one of the tall buildings, pointing and shouting.

Nokama rushed over to them. "What is it? What's happening?"

"It's Vhisola!" one shouted. "On top of that building! She's going to fall!"

The Toa of Water looked up. There was Vhisola, teetering on the edge of a roof. The Matoran wasn't going to be able to maintain her balance for long. Nokama felt helpless. She wasn't a climber, she could never scale the building in time.

She turned and leaped into the canal, extending her hydro blades in front of her. Her momentum carried her forward, skiing across the surface of the canal. Just before reaching a bridge, Nokama dove beneath the surface. She sped through the winding protodermis pipe, down a grade, and back up at incredible velocity. Powered by her fear for Vhisola's life, she flew out of the end of the pipe and soared high into the air, angling her body so she would land on the same roof as the Matoran.

Vhisola saw her coming, rocked a little, and started to fall. Nokama swooped down, caught the Matoran with one arm and the edge of the roof with the other, and hauled them both to safety.

If she expected gratitude, she was disappointed. "You," said Vhisola. "I knew it would be you. Now that you're a Toa Metru, you'll just cast an even longer shadow over me."

"Vhisola, whatever you think, we can deal with it later. I need that Great Disk!"

"Everyone wants my disk," said Vhisola. "Some four-legged thing — not a Rahi, I don't know what it was — chased me through the streets. I had to hide up here to get away from him. I never should have paid attention to that note."

"What note?"

Vhisola produced two small tablets. On the first was a jumble of Matoran numbers, on the second a code key. "Here. Let's see if you can de-code it faster than I did."

It took Nokama a few long moments, but finally she was able to read the message. It said: "Beware. The Toa serve the Morbuzakh. They must not find the Great Disks. Meet me at the protodermis falls with your disk and I will keep it safe. Ahkmou."

Nokama suddenly felt very cold. "Come on, Vhisola. We need to have a long talk with some friends of mine."

Ask a Ga-Matoran or a Ko-Matoran, and they would say Ta-Metru was the harshest, least hospitable spot in all of Metru Nui. The searing heat of the forges and the Great Furnace, the heavy smell of molten protodermis, the constant sound of crafters hammering away — to Matoran from the quieter districts, Ta-Metru was a nightmare.

Vakama, Toa of Fire, would have agreed with that opinion right now, if he'd had a moment to think. Instead, he was diving and rolling to avoid white-hot protodermis flowing from a vat high above. An accidental overflow or leak was always bad news, but in this case, it was far worse than that.

Vakama glanced up. Yes, the Morbuzakh vines were still there, trying hard to rip the protodermis vat off its chain and hurl it to the ground. If they succeeded, there might not be much left of this section of Ta-Metru.

The Toa's mind raced. Morbuzakh vines had never been seen this far inside a metru. Protodermis vats on their way to a forge should never stall long enough for anything to grab hold of them. But both had happened, and just when Vakama arrived in search of a missing mask maker.

Ta-Matoran workers were running for cover. But if enough hot protodermis hit the ground, there would be no place to hide. It would burn through anything in its path unless Vakama found a way to stop it.

Right. Sounds easy, thought the new Toa Metru. *Only how do I do it? I can't keep ducking and dodging. The vat is too high up to reach by climbing. Not that the Morbuzakh will let me get close enough anyway. Unless . . .*

Matau had made fun of his choice of a disk launcher for a Toa tool. But right now, Vakama felt like it was the wisest decision he had ever made. He looked at the three-digit code on one of his disks. The first digit identified where it was made, the second its power, the third its power level. This was a level 5 freeze disk. Better still, the disk had been made in Ko-Metru, which meant it carried an extra surprise for the Mor-buzakh vines.

Vakama rolled, came up in a crouch, aimed, and let the disk fly. As he expected, the Mor-buzakh vines reacted instantly, swiping at the spinning object. But Ko-Metru disks were made to swerve at high speed to avoid any obstacle. The Morbuzakh grasped only empty air as the disk flew onto its target.

Impact! The disk hit the gears above the vat head on, freezing them solid and stopping the tilt. The vines snaked back up to the vat but re-coiled violently when they touched the ice.

Vakama took the hint. He launched an-other disk at one of the vines. When it struck, veins of frost began to travel the length of the blackened tendril. The other vines writhed fran-tically in the air, then all of them retreated back through a crack in the ground.

The Toa Metru of Fire let out a long sigh of

relief. The forge was safe, and more importantly, he had learned that Morbuzakh hated the cold. He was puzzling over what that might mean when the control room attendant came rushing over.

"That was . . . amazing!" said the Ta-Matoran. "I thought we had seen the last of the Toa when Lhikan disappeared. If you hadn't been here —"

"I did what I had to do," said Vakama quietly. He wasn't used to being seen as a hero and wasn't sure if he would ever feel comfortable about being one. "What happened? I thought that the vats never stopped moving."

"Come and see," said the attendant grimly. Vakama followed him into the forge control center. The foreman pointed to an ugly burn on one of the panels. "That's what happened. Some four-legged monster broke in and fried the controls with a burst of energy."

Vakama knelt down for a closer look. Some components had been damaged, but they could be repaired. That was not half as interesting as the scattered protodermis dust he saw on the floor near the damaged portion. He had seen dust like that once before, on a visit to Po-Metru, but this glittered in the light. It was only upon closer examination that he spotted the crushed Ko-Metru knowledge crystals mixed in with the dust.

The Toa Metru glanced up at the attendant. "I think I can fix this, if you can do a favor for me. I'm looking for a mask maker named Nuhrii. He wasn't at his home or at his forge. Have you seen him?"

"Yes. He was here this morning," the attendant replied. "He was looking for a Great Mask he made. It was tossed as flawed, but he said someone told him the mask was fine. He wanted to retrieve it before it went into the furnace for meltdown."

"Did he find it?"

"It's not here. Must still be on the reject pile, so I sent him over there. Nuhrii was talking pretty crazy, though. Said if he couldn't find the mask, he knew where there was a Kanoka disk that could make the greatest mask anyone had ever worn. I guess he's been working a little too hard."

"Yes, I guess so," Vakama replied, not at all convinced Nuhrii was crazy. More likely, the Matoran was walking into a trap — or getting ready to spring one.

The Toa of Fire thought hard as he walked. The walls of Nuhrii's home had been lined with tablets, souvenirs of his work. Each tablet showed an image of a Kanohi mask and the Kanoka disk from which it had been made. One of the tablets had been smashed on the floor, and a failed attempt made to put it back together.

The forge attendant had said Nuhrii had made a flawed mask. Vakama guessed it was the tablet featuring that mask that had been broken in anger. When Nuhrii heard the mask was in fact perfect, he tried to put the tablet back together before rushing off to find the Kanohi.

That still left a few questions. Who had discovered the mask was still a good one and notified Nuhrii? And was the note the Matoran had received the truth or simply bait to lure him into a trap?

Vakama hoped to find the answer at the huge, fenced-in lot just ahead. Its official name was Protodermis Reclamation Center, but to every mask maker in Ta-Metru, it was a grave-yard. No matter how many hours of work had gone into a mask, a single, tiny flaw could ruin it. Then it would be transported here, to sit on top of a pile of other broken, useless masks until it could be fed to the furnace and melted down. It was the one place no mask maker ever wanted to visit.

A single guard stood at the gate. The bored look on his face disappeared when he saw a Toa coming toward him. "Who are you?" he asked.

"I am Toa Vakama." It felt so strange to say it. "Toa Metru of Fire. I need to get inside."

"I'm sorry, but I have orders from Turaga Dume. No one is allowed in. I don't want trouble with the Vahki."

"But you let Nuhrii in, didn't you? He's in danger, and I have to find him. Please open the gate."

"I can't! I could lose my job."

Vakama frowned. This argument was taking too much time. The guard was obviously more afraid of the Vahki than he was of making a Toa angry. *And why wouldn't he be? No Toa would ever harm an innocent.*

"Then I will open it for you," the Toa of Fire said. Concentrating harder than he ever had in his life, Vakama willed a narrow jet of flame from his hand. In an instant it had melted the lock into slag. "You did your job. Now I have to try and do mine."

The yard was quiet. Vakama walked past piles of Kanohi masks and other artifacts, all waiting behind the fences for their time in the Great Furnace. Some looked perfect to the naked eye, their flaws visible only to a truly skilled crafter. Others were badly mangled.

So focused was he on scanning the damaged items that he almost tripped over something in his path. When he regained his footing, he saw it was a Mask of Shielding someone had left lying in the path. Vakama bent down and picked it up. It looked familiar somehow, but he couldn't quite place it.

Then it struck him. The angle of the mask, the ridges around the eyepieces . . . these were marks of Nuhrii's work. Was this the mask the Matoran had been seeking, now cast aside as if it were worthless?

"Everyone seems to want that Kanohi today," said a Matoran behind him. Vakama turned to see the reclamation center caretaker approaching. "Nuhrii was here looking for it just a short while ago."

"But he didn't take it with him?" asked Vakama. "Why not?"

"Look for yourself. That mask has a hairline crack in the base," the caretaker replied, pointing to a barely visible flaw. "I've been doing this so long I can spot a bad one from a long way away. Mask maker must have cooled it too fast. Anyway, Nuhrii took one look at it, threw it down, and left. He was muttering something about forging the most powerful Kanohi ever made and showing up some other crafter. Vakama, I think his name was."

Me? Why would he want to outdo me? Vakama thought. *Sure, I had fewer masks wind up here, and Turaga Dume did ask me to craft a special Kanohi for him. But I never knew Nuhrii would be so jealous of that. After all, I learned so much from him.*

"I guess masks aren't the only things that can hide their flaws," the Toa of Fire said. "Do you have any idea where he's gone?"

The caretaker handed over a tablet. "He dropped this on his way out."

Vakama's eyes flew across the stone. There was no signature on the note, just some smudges of liquid protodermis. It read:

> *Nuhrii,*
> *Come to the abandoned mask maker's house in the northern reaches. You'll learn a valuable secret there — how to turn a Great*

Disk into a Kanohi mask that will live in legend. Come alone. Tell no one.

Vakama's mind reeled for a moment. He could see Nuhrii surrounded by shadowy tentacles that were reaching for him, grabbing him, squeezing the breath from the Matoran. Somehow, the Toa knew this danger was real, and it was happening now!

The caretaker watched Vakama race off and shook his head. Then he turned to the pile of broken masks and said, "Everyone's in such a hurry. Everyone except me . . . and all of you. We're in no rush to get where we're going, right?"

The Matoran laughed then, but Vakama was too far away to hear.

The Toa of Fire scanned his surroundings. He couldn't believe anything could make Nuhrii come here. This was a place no Ta-Matoran ever wandered, not if they hoped to see the twin suns rise again.

This had once been one of the most active sections of Ta-Metru. Vakama could remember riding the chutes here to see friends just a short time ago, but it seemed like ages had passed. Now the whole neighborhood was desolate and abandoned, surrendered to the power of the Morbuzakh. Half the buildings were reduced to rubble, and the rest did not look much better.

Vakama walked carefully, avoiding the chunks of solid protodermis that littered the street. Only the skittering of little Rahi among the wreckage broke the silence. Most of the Matoran who had lived here had fled, finding refuge with friends in the heart of the metru. Those who had chosen to stay were never seen or heard from again. Turaga Dume had declared the whole area off-limits, but soon found he did not need to dispatch Vahki to guard the place. No Matoran wanted to travel here.

Except Nuhrii, Vakama reminded himself. *But even if he is here, I may be too late to save him.*

As if in answer, a voice shouted, "Help!" It came from an abandoned crafter's home farther down the street. Vakama broke into a run, then stopped short when he saw the twin Morbuzakh vines slithering toward the same building. They were moving too quickly. He could never hope to outrace them.

"Help!"

Vakama loaded his last disk into the launcher and hoped he was making the right decision. He had never used this particular kind of disk before or even forged a mask from one. Its power was the least predictable and might make a bad situation worse. But there wasn't any other choice.

The disk shot through the air and struck the first vine, then began a sweeping arc that would bring it back to Vakama. On its way, it clipped the second vine, just as the Toa Metru had hoped it would. Before his eyes, both vines began to shimmer and fade. Then they were gone, teleported somewhere else in Metru Nui. Vakama hoped he had not just created a greater danger for someone else to deal with.

The door to the house was unlocked. As

soon as it was opened, a cloud of protodermis dust flew out, blinding and choking Vakama. When he could see again, he discovered the way in was blocked by rubble.

"Who's there? Help me! I'm trapped back here!" It was Nuhrii's voice, coming from somewhere beyond the pile of protodermis. The Morbuzakh vines had brought down the roof and were no doubt getting ready to start on the walls when the Toa Metru showed up.

For a moment, Vakama considered using his elemental power to melt through the obstacle. But his powers were so new, he had too little control over them. Make a mistake and the whole district might burn. No, he would have to do it the hard way, block by block.

Vakama removed one chunk of protodermis, but when he took out a second, the rubble shifted and more fell from the roof. "Hey, watch it!" Nuhrii shouted. "What are you trying to do?"

Vakama began again, proceeding more carefully. He shifted a block, paused, shifted it some more, until he was certain it wouldn't cause a collapse. It took a lot of careful work, but he finally managed to create a big enough opening for Nuhrii to crawl through. The Matoran was coated in dust but did not seem hurt.

"I thought I would never get out of there," said Nuhrii. Then he looked up at his rescuer for the first time. "Vakama! You!"

"Are you all right? What were you doing here?"

"Okay, why shouldn't I tell you? I came here to learn how to turn a Great Disk into a Mask of Power you could never dream of making. Then I would be the one others came to for the important Kanohi."

In all the time Vakama had worked as a mask maker, he had never once raised his voice. It had been Nuhrii who first hired him as a mask-making apprentice, and Nuhrii who had taught him the basic skills. But now, as Vakama thought of all he had been through to find the Matoran, he felt anger rise in him.

"Look around you, Nuhrii," the Toa said harshly. "Look at what the Morbuzakh has done to our city! This is no time to be thinking of personal glory. Everyone has to work together to stop this menace. That Great Disk you have is the key to saving Metru Nui. I don't know how, but it is. You have to tell me where to find it!"

Nuhrii looked shocked. It took him a moment before he could speak, but when he did, his tone was that of a Matoran ashamed. "The Great Disk? I — I didn't know. Yes, I will gladly help you find it."

The two left the house and started walking out of the abandoned zone. Although Nuhrii spoke under his breath, Vakama could hear him saying, "We'll get the disk. We'll stop the Morbuzakh. And everyone will know that I saved Metru Nui!"

The Toa Metru of Fire could only shake his head and walk on.

Whenua stood before the south gate of the Onu-Metru Archives, about at the end of his patience. "All right. For the fourth time, I am Whenua. I worked here my whole life. I need to get inside and find Tehutti before he does something we are all going to regret a whole lot."

He waited for an answer from the gate guard, who did not look impressed by the sight of a Toa Metru of Earth. Whenua considered finding another access to the Archives, but given that they covered almost the entire metru, it could be a long chute ride to another gateway. And there was no guarantee the guard there would be any more cooperative.

"Okay, you look like a Toa," said the guard. "But not any Toa I've ever seen. And Whenua? Whenua is an archivist, and he sure doesn't carry twin drills like yours. If you don't want to give me your real name, fine, but I can't let just anyone in here."

Whenua did his best to hold his temper. It would take too long to explain about how artifacts called Toa stones transformed six Matoran into Toa Metru, even assuming the guard would believe that. Even more frustrating was the fact that his Great Mask of Power might prove a help here, but he didn't even know what that power might be yet.

"Can you at least tell me if Tehutti is here?"

The guard chuckled. "Tehutti's always here, Toa 'Whenua.' He spends his whole life down with the exhibits. He showed up here all excited about some shipment or another, probably another Rahi only its mother could love. But there's nothing on the ship schedule for today."

Whenua frowned. When he had first found out Tehutti was missing, he went to the archivist's home. There he found a note offering an exotic Rahi for the Archives in exchange for a Great Disk. The note featured a crude drawing of the Rahi and was signed by a Ga-Metru Matoran named Vhisola. From the sound of things, Tehutti had rushed right over to make the exchange.

The Toa Metru of Earth made his decision. He pushed past the guard and went to the doorway. "Call the Vahki if you want to, I have to get in there. Now where did they hide those levers today?"

While the guard protested, Whenua ran his hands over the surface of the doorway. The Archives boasted a unique security system. Each door had three hidden levers whose location was changed every day. They had to be thrown in the right combination for the door to open, and that changed every day, too. Every Onu-Matoran believed it to be the perfect protection against intruders.

"Go ahead," said the guard. "No one has ever made it past that door. You won't stand a —"

Whenua threw the levers, one, two, three. The great door opened with a hiss. The Toa of Earth turned toward the guard and said, "What was that? Couldn't hear you over the door opening."

*   *   *

To Whenua, the Onu-Metru Archives were more than a storehouse or a museum. In his eyes, they were more magnificent than the crystal Knowledge Towers of Ko-Metru, the Great Temple, and the sculpture fields of Po-Metru all put together. The main floors extended for a great distance in every direction, and when they had taken up most of the space in the metru, work had begun on the lower levels and subbasements. The Archives now occupied the subterranean depths of the city, extending far beyond the boundaries of Onu-Metru.

Nor could it be said that the Archives were "finished." As more exhibits were added, Onu-Matoran workers continued to dig deeper and deeper down to find space to house them. Over time, they and the archivists had become so accustomed to the dim light underground that the brightness of the twin suns was hard on their eyes.

On the outside, the Archives looked grim and imposing. Inside, it was a vast treasure trove of every creation that had ever walked Metru

Nui. Rather than the dry historical records and prophecies of Ko-Metru, this was a living museum. Every Rahi beast, every insectlike Bohrok, every creature in the Archives was part of a living record. Inside their protodermis stasis tubes, they were alive but suspended in time forever.

Whenua walked into the first of the Rahi wings, enjoying the familiar scents of the Archives. He nodded a greeting to one of the oldest exhibits, a Nui-Rama captured in flight whose stasis chamber hung from the ceiling high above. All around, archivists scurried back and forth pushing their transport carts. These were used for moving exhibits of all sizes through the subterranean, protodermis-lined tunnels.

Whenua turned and headed for Tehutti's pride and joy, an exhibit of a Kane-Ra bull. Before he had even walked through the archway, he could see something was wrong. The section looked like a live Rahi had passed through, shattering the display case and scattering artifacts. Fortunately, only the outer shell had been broken. Had the inner casing been cracked, the Rahi inside might well have come to life again and rampaged through the Archives.

Whenua spotted Tehutti's transport cart in a corner, empty. Lying near it was a hammer, the kind used in Ta-Metru forges. The archivist in Whenua was dismayed. Ta-Metru artifacts belonged on one of the sublevels, not in a Rahi section. It was only when he looked again at all the damage that he realized why the hammer was there.

Who would want to sabotage these relics? he wondered. *Someone from Ta-Metru? Why?*

Shrugging, Whenua moved on to the next exhibit hall. Here were more Rahi, even larger ones, and carvings of those that had either eluded capture or whose displays had been moved into storage. The Toa Metru of Earth was looking for anything out of place, when one carving caught his eye. It depicted a massive Rahi with four legs and a long, muscular tail, ideal for striking out at opponents. Carved underneath the picture were the words "Nui-Jaga. Found in Po-

Metru, near the Sculpture Fields." Beside that was the name of the carver, Ahkmou.

A Nui-Jaga, he thought. *A Po-Metru Rahi. But this is the same beast Vhisola offered in trade for the Great Disk!*

As an archivist, Whenua was skilled at starting from the present and working back. No Ga-Matoran would even know what a Nui-Jaga was, most likely, let alone have one captive to trade. The offer to Tehutti had been a fake, probably written by someone other than this Vhisola. It was bait to get Tehutti to the Archives so the Great Disk could be stolen from him!

That thought made him realize something even worse. Whoever was trying to get the Great Disks — possibly that four-legged hunter Vakama talked about — might be right here in the Archives, planning an ambush. For a moment, he wondered if he should try to find help. Maybe a Toa, or even the Vahki . . .

Then he remembered — he *was* a Toa. It was his job to face danger and overcome it. And nothing — *nothing!* — would make him risk the safety of his Archives or his city.

He ran for the nearest exit to the outer dock. Still getting used to his new, far more powerful form, he stumbled a few times and almost crashed into a display of parasitic krana. With a shudder, he kept going, thanking the Great Beings he had not set those *things* loose.

Any shipment, no matter how large or small, had to come through the outer dock. The Matoran who worked here were both smart and brave. It was their job to make sure every "exhibit" was ready to be placed in a stasis tube, where its life processes would be slowed to a crawl. If one of the creatures intended for archiving decided to wake up, it would be up to the dockworkers to put it back to sleep again.

When Whenua arrived on the dock, a four-Matoran crew was trying to subdue a Gukko bird long enough for it to be put in stasis and archived. The powerful winged beast was objecting. There was about a fifty-fifty chance it would break away and head for the sky, carrying a Matoran or two with it.

Whenua went over to help, but the dock leader got in the way. "We have to do it ourselves," said the Matoran. "Understand? If we start depending on a Toa, what happens when you're not around?"

Whenua looked from the dock leader to the crew and back again. Then he nodded. "Okay, then — for now. Have you seen Tehutti?"

"He was headed for the next dock over. I told him not to waste his time. This Rahi was a last-minute find, but there aren't any others on the schedule. And nothing from any Vhisola."

"I know. I'm pretty sure he knows, too," replied Whenua, turning away. "Make sure that Gukko's fast asleep. Last time one got loose, it brought down half the exhibits in sublevel three."

"How did you know about that?" the dock leader asked. But the Toa of Earth was already gone.

*　　*　　*

Whenua pounded around the corner. All he could think about was finding Tehutti in time and stopping him from doing something the whole city would regret later. He scanned for any sign of the Matoran or for signs of a trap.

What he found was a well-concealed hole with a narrow ladder leading down into darkness. On a hunch, he began to climb down. He had made it about halfway when a rung gave way beneath his foot.

The next thing he knew, he was falling. And falling. Down, down, into the sublevels and sub-sublevels of the Archives, and then farther still, thinking to himself all the while: *Stupid. Stupid, stupid, stupid!*

Thoughts rushed through his mind. Was this the trap set for Tehutti, and had the Matoran already fallen into it? Just how far down did this pit go? And could even a Toa survive such a plunge?

Whenua found out an instant later, when he came to a crashing halt far below the lowest levels of the Archives. Despite spending a lifetime working here, even he had never been this far down before. But he had heard rumors of a level far below the surface, where exhibits that had proven potentially dangerous were placed for safekeeping.

The Toa Metru of Earth sat up and groaned. His bruises had bruises and his head was pounding. With a great deal of effort, he rose.

The hallways down here were even darker and more narrow than the ones above. Lightstones were few and far between. Anyone who came down here left in a hurry, so why waste illumination?

He had only taken three steps when he heard the sound every archivist dreads. It was a unique crunch, the sound of stasis-tube fragments being crushed underfoot.

Whenua forced himself to remain calm. *So one of the cases was broken, so what? Maybe it's only the outer shell that was damaged, and there's nothing to worry about. Yes, it had to be the outer shell, because if it was the inner shell, then something would be loose down here. Something very nasty.*

He had seen it happen before. Outer shells could take all kinds of pounding, but if the inner shell of a stasis tube cracked even a little, the rush of air would wake up the contents. When the contents had teeth, claws, and a hatred of being caged up, this generally turned out to be a bad thing.

Whenua did his best to move quietly down the corridor, not easy with his large frame. He reminded himself that he had been an experienced Onu-Metru archivist before becoming a Toa. As a Matoran, he had faced down his share of snarling Rahi. What could be down here that could possibly bother him now?

The answer came with twin beams of pure, blazing heat that creased the side of his Kanohi mask. The wall of the corridor sizzled where they struck, and the hallway was suddenly filled with the smell of charred protodermis. Whenua whirled to see a Rahkshi heading right toward him, red eyes gleaming in its hideous yellow face.

Startled, he found he could not remember the creature's exact name. But he didn't have to strain to recall its power — heat vision, capable of burning a hole through anything, including newly created Toa. No one was quite certain just where Rahkshi came from, but everyone wished they had stayed there.

Whenua ducked another heat blast and darted into another corridor. He needed time to think and space to maneuver, neither of which the Rahkshi was likely to give him. This would be a great time to use his Kanohi Mask of Power, if only he knew what it did. The twin earthshock drills he carried could punch their way through almost anything, and his elemental power . . .

Yes, that was it. When he reached the far end of the hall, he activated the drills and began tearing up the flooring. His elemental power would affect the earth underneath, but there was no harm giving it a little help.

The Rahkshi turned the corner and started toward him, its powerful body gleaming in the dim light. He could hear the horrible screech of the kraata it carried inside. Twin shafts of red shot toward him from the Rahkshi's eyes, Whenua barely moving aside in time. Then it was the moment to go to work.

The Toa Metru looked down and did his best to ignore the advancing creature. He willed the earth to rise, to form an impenetrable wall between him and the Rahkshi. He could see the soil beginning to shift, running together and then swirling as if mini cyclones had taken hold.

It was a toss-up who was more shocked by what happened next, the Rahkshi or Whenua. A mound of earth suddenly rose from the floor, hardening rapidly and blocking the creature from coming closer. Whenua took a step back and smiled, imagining how the other Toa would feel when he told them about this. Nuju probably couldn't even manage an icicle, or Onewa move a pebble, or . . .

The celebration came to an abrupt end. Twin red spots appeared on the earth wall, glowing brighter and brighter every moment. While Whenua had been patting himself on the back, the Rahkshi was focusing its power to melt the obstacle in its path.

Okay, maybe I won't tell the others about this, Whenua decided.

He ducked into a doorway just as the wall crumbled. There was something Tehutti had said about yellow Rahkshi once, if only he could remember. What was it? Tehutti was always on about one piece of exhibit trivia or another.

Then it came to him. Right after it uses its heat beams, the Rahkshi's eyesight is weakened temporarily. Tehutti had been right, too, for the creature walked right past Whenua's hiding place without spotting him.

Once the Rahkshi was gone, Whenua fought a strong urge to get out of the Archives. Then he remembered that Tehutti might well be down here, and if he was, the Rahkshi would find him. Like it or not, he had to go on.

But maybe I don't have to fight the Rahkshi, he realized. *Not if I can get something else to do it for me.*

Whenua raced down the hallway, stopping only long enough to pry a lightstone out of the wall. By its beam, he was able to spot the shattered Rahkshi stasis tube. He scooped up as many of the inner casing fragments as he could find, then went back on the trail of the creature.

As he walked, he tried to remember everything he could about this level. Over time, he had seen a number of exhibits sent down here, even marked a few for storage himself. If he was correct, all he had to do was find the right one.

It took a lot of walking, numerous twists and turns, and a few potentially dangerous mistakes before Whenua spotted the door he wanted. It was one of the few down here that had a sign, which read DANGER: MUAKA PEN. He could hear the great Rahi cat pacing and growling behind the door. Food was sent down to it once a day from the upper levels through a small chute, but Muaka were notorious for always being hungry. Better still, they did not get along with Rahkshi at all.

Whenua took a deep breath. This was going to be tricky. First, he scattered the protodermis fragments on the floor in front of the door. Then he used his earthshock drill to punch a hole through the lock. He waited until he could hear the Muaka charging before he dove for cover.

The door crashed open. The huge Rahi snarled, sniffing the air and snapping its massive jaws together. Whenua watched anxiously as the Muaka lowered its head and picked up the scent off the fragments. The beast's eyes narrowed at the smell of Rahkshi, and it took off at a run.

Whenua followed. Letting another creature loose down here went against his nature as an archivist, but it would be easier to cage the Muaka again than a Rahkshi. He just had to hope the Muaka found the Rahkshi before either found Tehutti.

He was deep in the heart of the storage level when he heard the snarls up ahead. The sounds were followed by red flashes of heat vision, then an impact that shook the entire section. The Muaka had tracked down his prey.

Whenua rounded the corner to see Rahi and Rahkshi locked in a mighty struggle. Ordinarily, the Rahkshi would be the clear favorite, but the Muaka's bulk reduced his foe's room to maneuver. Beyond them, the Toa could see an open chamber where Tehutti strained to get out from under a pile of artifacts.

The Toa forced himself to wait for the right moment. When Muaka lifted his right forepaw to strike, Whenua dove, slid across the floor past the two creatures, and ended up in the same chamber as the Matoran.

"Get me out of here!" Tehutti cried. "I'll do anything!"

Whenua worked quickly and carefully, pushing the debris aside and hoping the struggle outside would go on a little longer. "Anything? Then how about giving me that Great Disk you have while there's still a city up above to save."

Tehutti shrugged off the last few pieces of Metru Nui history and nodded. "I never thought I would be glad to see you. I fell down here, and some four-legged Rahi bait demanded I give him the disk. When I wouldn't do it, he brought this stuff down on me and left me here. You want the disk? You can have it. I'd rather be trapped in a broken chute with a horde of Vahki than hold on to it now!"

Whenua glanced out into the hall, made sure Rahi and Rahkshi were still busy, then slammed the door and locked it. "We'll have to dig a new tunnel to get out of here. In the meantime, you can explain why you ever thought a Ga-Matoran would have a Nui-Jaga to trade for the disk."

Tehutti watched in awe as Whenua's earthshock drills went to work on the wall. "I — I knew she wouldn't. My friend Ahkmou told me all about Nui-Jaga long ago, so I knew they didn't come from Ga-Metru. I wanted to see why someone wanted the Great Disk . . . and if they really did have a Nui-Jaga, well . . ."

"You would have traded the city's safety for a new exhibit to put your name on," Whenua replied.

"With you for a Toa Metru, Whenua, how safe is the city now?" Tehutti said. "Besides, nothing very bad is going to happen to Metru Nui. Turaga Dume will figure out some way to deal with the Morbuzakh and everything will be fine."

"I hope so." Whenua powered down his drills. He had managed to punch a good-size hole in the wall. On the other side was another darkened corridor with a distinct upward slope. Hopefully, it led to the main floors.

"Let's go," said the Toa of Earth. "We have a long journey ahead. If we run into the Morbuzakh, make sure to tell it that it's not a threat. I've never seen a plant laugh before."

The Matoran put down his tools and stood very still. He had heard two sets of footsteps behind him, heavy footsteps, and he really did not want to turn around and see who it might be.

"Well, well, well," hissed a too-familiar voice. "Here I am again."

The Matoran forced himself to look. Yes, it was Nidhiki again, this time accompanied by a hulking brute with energy crackling from his hands.

"I came back to get the Great Disks," Nidhiki continued. "You know, the ones I want *very badly*? The ones you promised to get for me?"

"I — I don't have them. Not yet," the Matoran stammered. "But I'll get them! It's just taking a little more time than I thought."

"I see," Nidhiki replied. He gestured with one of his legs, and his lumbering companion moved toward the Matoran. "This is my friend. He doesn't like Matoran. He particularly doesn't like you."

The Matoran looked up at the bestial face of the brute who towered over him. "I'm doing my best! Really!"

"Your best?" Nidhiki repeated. "Three of the Toa are close to finding the Great Disks. Your efforts to trap the Matoran and divert the Toa Metru have been failures. Do you know what that means?"

The Matoran swallowed hard as the two creatures crowded close to him. "N-n-no."

"It means you're going to do better than your best. I've been to Ko-Metru and arranged to keep Toa Nuju busy. I expect you to arrange a little surprise for Toa Matau and get the Le-Metru disk. I know you aren't foolish enough to disappoint me again, are you?"

The Matoran shook his head. He wanted to say something, but his mouth didn't seem to be working.

"Good. Then I hope the next time I see you, you will have all six Great Disks for me. But either way," Nidhiki added smiling, "it will be the last time I see you, Matoran. Understand?"

The two left before the Matoran could answer. They were barely out the door before he gathered up his things and headed for the chute station. He had an appointment in Le-Metru that he wouldn't miss if his life depended on it.

And it sounds like it does! the Matoran thought as he dashed out into the street.

6

From high atop a gleaming Knowledge Tower, Nuju looked down upon the landscape of Ko-Metru. For the Toa Metru of Ice, this was a most unusual vantage point. Normally, his eyes were on the sky, seeking to read the future from the brightness and movement of the stars.

But if Vakama was right, there might not be much of a future for Metru Nui if the Great Disks were not found. It was true that the Morbuzakh plant had done some pretty serious damage to the metru. Still, Nuju was not sure just how far he wished to trust the Toa of Fire's "visions."

Down below, all was still and silent. Even the hum of the transport chutes that carried Matoran from place to place was muted here. Nothing was allowed to disturb the work of the Matoran scholars who toiled in the crystal

Knowledge Towers. There they pored over the written records of Metru Nui, deciphered ancient prophecies, and crafted predictions of the future. Once, Nuju had been one of them. Now it was up to him to make sure there would be tomorrows to ponder.

At first, it seemed like that would be a simple enough task. The Ko-Metru Matoran who Vakama claimed had knowledge of the disk was named Ehrye. Finding him should not have been an issue. In fact, it was often impossible *not* to find Ehrye, even when you wanted to avoid him. He was constantly underfoot, running errands for different scholars and pleading for a chance to become one of them.

Nuju, naturally, had said no. Working in a Knowledge Tower required wisdom, patience, and experience. All Ehrye had to offer were enthusiasm and too much energy for his own good. So the Matoran went back to running errands and dreaming of life inside the towers.

And now, when I want to find him, he's disappeared! fumed Nuju.

A search of Ehrye's home had turned up a marked Ko-Metru chute station map and a disturbing journal entry. It read in part:

> *I'm going to show them. If I turn over the Great Kanoka Disk like I said I would, I'll learn a secret that will make them beg me to join a Knowledge Tower!*

Nuju shook his head. He had spent his whole life studying what might be and what would be in the days to come, and he knew one thing for certain. There was no future in what Ehrye was about to do.

The Toa of Ice leaped from the top of a Knowledge Tower, his eyes focused on the ledge of another. When he had maneuvered within arm's reach of it, he snapped a crystal spike from his back and swung it hard. It dug into the side of the tower. Nuju swung gracefully around the building, pulling the spike free as he did so. He repeated the exercise twice more on the way down, growing more used to his new Toa tools along the way. Someday, he knew, that experience might save his life.

Nuju had taken the chute map with him when he left Ehrye's house. He hit the ground close to the station that was marked on the map. The attendant was deep in thought and did not notice his approach.

"What? Oh!" he exclaimed when Nuju tapped his shoulder. "Who are you? What do you want?"

"I am Nuju, Toa Metru of Ice. I am looking for a runner named Ehrye. Have you seen him?"

The attendant frowned. "Yes, he was here. I saw him talking to a Matoran from another metru. I don't remember which. Then he jumped in a chute heading for one of the Knowledge Towers. He was muttering something about a disk."

"Where did he have this conversation?"

"Ummm . . . Let me see. I remember I was analyzing chute dynamics at the time and not really paying attention. But I think it was in that corner over there."

Nuju turned away without saying thank you. He was in no mood to waste words. Instead, he walked over to where the attendant had directed him and looked around. There was little to be seen, just a Po-Metru carving tool and a pass to the Onu-Metru Archives. Either might be important, or they might have been dropped by any of hundreds of Matoran who passed through this chute station.

The attendant had gone back to pondering. It was something Ko-Metru Matoran spent a lot of time doing, in hopes of one day securing a position in a Knowledge Tower. Unfortunately, it also made it hard to get their attention.

"If you see Ehrye again, hold on to him," Toa Nuju said.

"Hmmm? What? Hold on to whom?" the attendant asked, confused.

Nuju walked away, wondering why he even bothered to talk to some Matoran.

The chute Ehrye had taken led to the lower level of a Knowledge Tower. It was such a silent place it made the rest of the metru seem positively wild and loud. A small number of Ko-Matoran were hard at work, junior seers who hoped to one day ascend to the ranks of those who labored on the upper levels. Nuju had spent most of his life in Knowledge Towers and could not recall ever seeing a group of scholars looking so annoyed.

As usual, trying to get a scholar to take a break from his studies to talk was like trying to teach kolhii rules to a Rahkshi. They did not seem at all impressed by the presence of a Toa Metru. It was only when Nuju mentioned that a Great Disk was involved that one of them agreed to talk.

"A Great Disk, hmmm?" said the scholar. "Incredible power. I would love the chance to study one. Do you have it?"

"No, I am seeking it. I believe a Matoran named Ehrye is as well, and he may have come here."

"Ehrye!" the scholar spat. "So that was his name! He barged in asking a lot of questions about Kanoka disks, the Morbuzakh plant, and other things that were not his business. No, not his business at all! Then he took a chute to the top of the tower, which is forbidden!"

The other Matoran had turned to see what all the shouting was about. The scholar spotted their angry looks and dropped his voice almost to a whisper. "You will find him there, but you must do something for us in exchange for this information."

The scholar dug into his robes and pulled out a knowledge crystal a little larger than Nuju's hand. "The Morbuzakh vines have done great damage to our towers," the scholar explained. "With this crystal, a new tower can be grown. When you reach the top level, throw this into the air. Wherever it lands, a new tower shall appear."

Nuju took the crystal. "A gift to the future of Metru Nui, then. I will do it."

High atop the Knowledge Tower, the air was crisp and clean. One could always find a sense of peace and the time for contemplation here.

What could not be found, at least today, was any sign of Ehrye.

Toa Nuju felt the weight of the crystal in his hand. He approached the edge of the tower, took a deep breath, and tossed the crystal out into space. It tumbled through the air, vanishing into the mist below. An instant later, Nuju followed.

As he fell, he let doubt creep into his mind again. What if Vakama was wrong? What if the Great Disks proved to no one that they were Toa? What if the Great Disks didn't exist at all but were just legends? What then?

Nuju twisted his body in midair. He could barely see the outlines of the new tower. An instant later, he landed feetfirst on the top of the rapidly growing structure. It lifted him high in the air once more as it took its place among the other monuments to knowledge in Ko-Metru.

From this new vantage point, Nuju scanned the metru. Off to the west, he spotted something that looked out of place. A Knowledge Tower's rooftop was littered with protodermis blocks.

Since towers were grown, not built, there was no reason any construction material would be there.

He was about to dismiss it as one more strange thing in a city that seemed to be filled with them when he spotted movement behind the blocks. It was Ehrye! Nuju had barely realized that when he saw something much more frightening — a huge crack traveling up the side of the tower. The whole structure was about to fragment and take the Matoran with it.

Nuju got a running start and leaped off the tower. Using his crystal spikes, he swung from one chute to the next as fast as he could. When he was almost on top of the tower, he let go and dropped.

For once, the Toa of Ice tried not to think about the future. If he pondered the possible consequences of what he was trying to do, he would never be able to do it. He waited until his fall had brought him almost parallel to the crack in the tower, then held out his twin spikes and focused his ice power through them. Thin streams of ice shot from the tools, welding the crack shut as he fell.

Now came the hard part. Most of the damage was repaired, but if he could not stop his fall, he would be an ex–Toa Metru very quickly. He spun, twisted, and dug one spike into the side of the tower. It carved a gash in the crystal and he continued to fall, desperately trying to hang on to the Toa tool. Finally, with the ground much too close for comfort, the spike held and he came to an abrupt stop.

No wonder we had to be chosen to be Toa Metru, he thought as he began the long climb to the top of the tower. *No one would ever volunteer for this job.*

Ehrye was still where Nuju had last seen him: trapped behind protodermis blocks at the very top of the tower. Worse, the blocks had not been stacked haphazardly. They were arranged, almost like a puzzle, in such a way that moving the wrong one would bring them all crashing down on the Matoran.

Nuju spent a long time staring at the blocks before he gently shifted one. Then he went back to analyzing the barricade. Ehrye, impatient, shouted, "Are you going to get me out of here? What are you doing?"

"Quiet," Nuju replied. "Someone did not want you walking away from this tower. But you are important to the future of Metru Nui, fortunately for you, so the Toa of Ice is going to get you out of what you have gotten into."

"Yes, I heard you were a Toa," said the Matoran grimly. "Now I'll never have a chance at a promotion."

The Toa Metru ignored him. This puzzle was highly intricate, but it was designed to defeat someone who could not think ahead. *They picked the wrong Toa then,* Nuju said to himself.

It took an agonizingly long time, but finally enough blocks were cleared for Ehrye to slip out. He stretched himself and looked up at his rescuer. "I suppose you're wondering how I got here?"

"Yes. You took many risks, Ehrye, and broke a number of laws. I should turn you over to the

Vahki and be done with it. But I need you. Or, rather, I need the Kanoka disk you have located."

"Why should I give it to you?" Ehrye replied. "That disk could be my ticket to a Knowledge Tower position."

Nuju gestured at the pile of protodermis blocks. "It was almost your ticket to a tomb. Think about the future, Ehrye."

The Matoran spent a few minutes doing just that. Then he said, "I get full credit for finding it? And no Vahki come knocking on my door?"

"Vahki don't knock," Nuju reminded him. "They smash doors down. And they keep smashing them down until they find the one you're hiding behind."

"You have a point," Ehrye agreed. "Even if I didn't have to worry about them, there's still that big Rahi breath that walled me up here."

Nuju and Ehrye headed for the chute that would bring them back down to ground level. Still shaken by his experience, Ehrye wouldn't stop babbling. "I know why you're looking for that disk, Toa Nuju. It's the root, right?"

"Root?"

"The Morbuzakh plant — it has a king root. I found that out when I was researching the Great Disk. Stop the root, you stop the spread of the plant. But you need all six disks to do it."

"Then you will come with me to see the other Toa Metru now," Nuju said.

"There are more of you?"

"And then we will go get the Great Disk."

"Oh, I'll tell you where it is. I'll even go with you. But you're going to have to retrieve it. From what I've learned, no one but a Toa Metru has a chance of getting that disk from its hiding place."

"I see," Nuju said.

"In fact," continued Ehrye, "I might not get the Knowledge Tower job. But if the Great Disk is as hard to get as I think it is, your job might be open soon, Toa of Ice."

Neither one of them laughed at Ehrye's little joke.

* * *

When they reached the ground, Nuju gestured for Ehrye to follow him. To the Matoran's surprise, they did not head for a chute station but for the alley behind the tower.

"Where are we going?"

"Knowledge Towers do not crack by themselves," said Nuju. "Well, sometimes they do, but this one did not. I am searching for the cause."

Ehrye trailed along behind as Nuju walked up and down the length of the alley. Along the way, the Matoran peppered him with questions. "What are you looking for? Does that mean anything? What does it feel like to be a Toa Metru? Do you think the Morbuzakh plant will wreck the whole city?"

"Enough!" Nuju snapped. "The future will bring the answers to your questions, but only if you stop speaking long enough to notice them."

"That's what you always say," Ehrye grumbled.

"When it stops being true, I will stop saying it," Nuju replied.

The Toa of Ice moved around to a shadowed portion of the tower. There, just below eye level, was the beginning of the crack that had threatened to bring the whole structure down. Peering closely at it, he looked for any sign of the tool that had been used.

What he found was something quite different. The edges of the damaged area were melted and fused. In many places, the crystal had turned black. No Matoran tool had done this. It was a surge of energy.

Troubled, Nuju knelt down to examine the ground. Crushed knowledge crystals littered the pavement. The Toa of Ice carefully sifted through them to reveal scrapings on the ground below. They were the marks of a four-footed being who had stood right in that spot while he no doubt set his trap.

Vakama was right, Nuju thought. *This time. But who is this monster? Why is he doing this? Is he working for someone else, or does he stand to gain somehow by all this damage?*

He rose and walked toward the mouth of

the alley, not saying a word to Ehrye. The Matoran kicked at the knowledge crystal fragments before following. His thoughts had gone back to the missed opportunity of the Great Disk. If he could have gotten his hands on it or maybe somehow tricked Nuju into getting it for him, Ko-Metru would have been at his feet. Now it would be back to running errands. Unless, of course, he could still find a way to get the disk after Nuju found it.

Ehrye was still pondering that happy thought when Nuju stopped short. The Toa of Ice bent down to pick up an artifact, but Ehrye could not make out what it was. After a moment, Nuju turned around and held the item out. It was a small, intricate carving.

"What's that?" Ehrye asked.

"I thought perhaps you could tell me," said Nuju coldly. "This came from Po-Metru. It's signed by Ahkmou the carver."

Ehrye shrugged. "So?"

"At the chute station, the attendant said he saw you talking with a Matoran before you left for the Knowledge Tower. He couldn't remember who it was, but I think I know. It was Ahkmou, wasn't it? That's why there was a Po-Metru carving tool in the station. He was careless... must have been in a big hurry."

"Okay, so it was Ahkmou," Ehrye replied. "We're friends. We play kolhii together sometimes. What does this have to do with —?"

"Listen to me," Nuju said, leaning in so close that Ehrye was chilled by his frigid breath. "We are not playing kolhii now. All of Metru Nui is at stake. Now, what did Ahkmou want?"

Ehrye broke and ran. Nuju frowned and used a minimal amount of elemental power to block the alley with a wall of ice. Stymied, the Matoran turned around.

"Wrong answer," said Nuju.

"All right. He said he wanted to carve replicas of the Great Disks as a gift for Turaga Dume. He wanted to know all about them and figured I could get information from the Knowledge Towers."

"Is that all he said?"

"Yes," Ehrye answered, his eyes on the ground.

Nuju could tell he was not revealing the whole truth, but there would be time to uncover it later. For now, they needed to return to Ga-Metru and meet with the other Toa. He turned and walked toward the chute station, confident that Ehrye would be wise enough not to try to run again.

"What are you going to do about that ice wall?" the Matoran asked. "Will it melt?"

"Eventually."

"Won't there be questions? I mean, how many Matoran know there's a Toa of Ice around?"

"It will give the scholars something to ponder," said Nuju. "And before all is said and done, all of Metru Nui will know that Toa Nuju has arrived."

Matau, Toa Metru of Air, knew all about chutes. He had been riding the transparent, magnetized protodermis tubes from place to place all his life, as had most Matoran. Living in Le-Metru, transport hub for the entire city, he had even had the chance to repair a chute or three in his time. He was quite proud of the fact that no one outside of his metru knew more about chutes than he did.

All of which made it even stranger that he was now hurtling out of control through a chute at a ridiculously high speed, heading for what would probably be a very dead end.

Outside the chute, the green-and-brown structures of Le-Metru were nothing but a blur. Matau whipped around a corner, heading for a busy junction and hoping he was not about to collide with some poor Matoran. For at least the tenth time, he tried to jump through the walls of the chute and exit. But he was thrown back yet again, slamming into the opposite wall and then picking up speed again.

I wanted to get there quick-fast, but not this quick-fast, he thought. He wasn't sure how anyone could manage to seal off the walls of a chute, or whether this affected the entire metru system or just the tube he was rocketing through.

But I can take a smart-guess. Fire-spitter was right. These disks must be important, and someone doesn't want me to find mine.

Matau's mind raced almost as fast as his body through the chute. The chutes ran throughout the city, but the densest concentration was in Le-Metru. They all fed into one another. If it was only this chute that had been tampered with, then it should be possible to steer into another at the junction.

"Possible. Not healthy-safe, but possible," he muttered.

First thing Matau had to do was slow down. He unhooked his twin aero slicers from his back and tried digging them into the walls of the chute to act as brakes. But whatever had made the chute resist exits also made it too tough for the slicers to pierce.

I'm thought-planning like a Matoran still, Matau told himself. *The tools aren't the power. I'm a Toa-hero. I'm the power!*

The Toa Metru of Air glanced ahead. The junction was rushing up toward him, and a transport cart was heading for it from a side chute. At the rate he was moving, he would slam right into the cart. But if he could use his power to slow just a little . . .

Matau was not famous for deep thought and concentration, but he managed some now. He forced his will on the air in the chute, making it form a thick cushion to lower his speed. Little by little, he could feel himself slowing, but would it be enough?

The transport cart shot through the junction. A split second later, Matau went through. Straining, he reached out and grabbed the back of the cart, letting it pull him down the side chute.

The abrupt stop and change of direction almost ripped his arm out of the socket, but somehow he found the strength to hang on. It was only when he had traveled some way from his original chute that he let go and exited out the wall. Then he waited until the world around him stopped going in circles.

Toa Matau found himself not far from his original destination: the Ussal crab pen of the Le-Matoran named Orkahm. He decided to skip a chute and instead take the sky route via the cables that hung everywhere in Le-Metru.

Ussal pens could be found all over the metru. The carts they pulled transported goods too large or fragile for the chutes or carried Matoran who preferred to travel a little more slowly. The large crabs were specially trained to obey the commands of their riders, although they had been known to get temperamental at times. Even from high above, it was easy to locate an Ussal crab pen by the aroma — they were not the sweetest-smelling Rahi around.

Matau dropped to the ground near one of the crab keepers. "Don't worry-fear! It's me, Matau. I am a Toa-hero now!"

The keeper dropped his tools in surprise. "Wow! You've pulled some great jokes before, Matau, but this — this tops them all."

"This isn't a joke," Matau insisted. "I was given this Toa stone, and I brought it to the Great Temple, and . . . There isn't time for this. I am looking to seek-find Orkahm. Have you seen him?"

"No," the keeper said. "And I would just as soon he stays away. He's been acting crazy. Said he found something on his route-path, but wouldn't show it to anyone. He was going to bury-hide it. Orkahm always seemed like such a good rider. Who knew the pressure would get to him?"

Matau nodded. It would take too long to explain the situation, but he knew Orkahm had not lost his mind. The Matoran had found a Great Disk and knew someone would try to take it away from him, maybe the same someone who had sabotaged the chute. "So he's gone?"

"He is, but his cart's here. Why are you so interested, Matau? Planning a trick-joke on him?" the keeper said, laughing. "He already doesn't like you. I don't think you want to make it worse."

Matau spotted Orkahm's cart, sitting alone off to the side of the pens. Each rider kept a logbook of his travels during the day, and Orkahm was no exception. Matau fished it out from under the seat and flipped it open, only to discover the careful rider had written the whole thing in code.

Matau was tempted to give up. Then he reminded himself that the other Toa Metru had probably made contact with their Matoran and were waiting for him. He couldn't show up empty-handed. Besides, finding Orkahm and the disk would prove to everyone in Le-Metru that he was a Toa-hero.

He sat down on the cart and began studying the code. Matau had known Orkahm a long time. The Matoran was thorough, cautious, and meticulous, which made him a slow rider. Matau, on the other hand, had always been fast and reckless, which was why the two never got along.

But the most important thing Matau remembered about Orkahm was that he had little imagination.

Once the Toa realized that, breaking the code was simple. Orkahm had substituted numbers for letters, but it wasn't done in a particularly clever way. Deciphered, there were three entries, all dated the day before.

Disk hidden.

A. wants disk.

Moto-hub sector 3.

He's deephiding in sector 3, Matau realized. *He's either a fool or very, very scared. Probably both.*

Matau jumped in a chute headed northeast. Sector 3 was just across one of the major protodermis canals from Ta-Metru. It had long been known for the sheer number of chute malfunctions that took place there. These were blamed on everything from poor construction to just bad luck, until repair crews sent to the area started disappearing. That was when rumors began to spread that the Morbuzakh was behind all the troubles. Since then, all repair crews traveled with

Vahki escorts. Even with that, the Vahki usually returned alone. And since the security squads were incapable of speech, they couldn't explain what had happened.

If Orkahm wanted a place to hide, he chose a dangerous one, Matau thought. *Unless he thinks-knows something I don't?*

Matau leaped out of the chute at a station on the outskirts of the sector. The area had not been abandoned. There were still plenty of riders and other Matoran to be seen, hard at work. But everyone seemed to be moving very quickly and looking over their shoulders every few seconds. This part of Metru Nui wasn't ruled by Turaga Dume or the Vahki. It was ruled by fear.

The sudden appearance of a Toa in their midst drew a lot of attention from the Le-Matoran. They crowded around, asking questions, admiring his armor, and saying that now they were sure everything would be all right. Matau was having such a good time he almost forgot why he was there.

He was reminded abruptly when a transport

manager came up to him and said, "Are you looking for Orkahm?"

"Yes. How did you know?"

"He came hurry-running through here a little while ago. He said someone might be following him, and if anyone asked, not to tell them where he had gone."

"Then why are you telling me? Not that I am sad-complaining," said Matau.

"Because you are a Toa," the transport manager replied. "I have seen Toa before, a long time ago, but never met one. I know the legends, though — how Toa are here to protect us and keep us safe. Whatever Orkahm is doing, I don't think he's safe right now. Do you?"

Orkahm had made straight for a long-unused chute that went even deeper into sector 3. Matau was about to follow when he noticed something on the support struts beneath the chute. Something had been scratched into the solid protodermis.

Matau knelt down to take a closer look.

The carving was relatively fresh, made with a short, sharp instrument. It had left behind proto-dermis dust in the scratchings, but not dust from the strut. This looked more like dust from Po-Metru. Carved into the strut was a single word: PEWKU.

Matau read it once more to make sure he wasn't mistaken. Under ordinary circumstances, he would have dismissed this as some Matoran's idea of fun, leaving a mark behind on a chute. Matau had done that sort of prank himself in the past, along with hundreds of others.

But this was no joke — this was a message. Pewku was the name of Orkahm's favorite Ussal crab, the one he had been riding for as long as Matau could remember. The Toa doubted Orkahm would have taken the time to scratch this in the strut.

Someone else, then, he said to himself. *As a code-sign?*

Without hesitating even for a moment, Matau jumped into the chute and began to follow the trail of the missing Matoran.

*   *   *

The farther one traveled into this portion of Le-Metru, the more the buildings, chutes, and cables seemed to crowd in. The residents were fighting a losing battle against the Morbuzakh here. It was obvious that even the Vahki were not venturing this far, because Matau spotted at least two nests of insectoid Nui-Rama on rooftops. Normally, they would have been netted and shipped off to the Archives long ago.

Matau could see the chute change direction sharply up ahead. To his trained eye, it was obvious that the chute had not been built that way. Someone had rerouted it and not done a very good job. Still, the cylinder of energy held as he tore around the corner and went flying into the air.

Of course. Badly fix-patched chute, cut-severed end . . . why am I surprised?

He landed hard amid a tangled nest of transport cables. These cables helped feed energized protodermis into the chutes and chute stations, not to mention being great fun to swing from. Matau was puzzling over how he would ever untangle them when he noticed something in the center of the tangle, looking like it had been caught in a Fikou spiderweb.

It was Orkahm!

"Rider!" Matau said. "How did you get yourself in this trap-snare?"

"I didn't! Someone put me here!" the Matoran replied. "Now, please get me out!"

Matau worked as quickly as he could, unknotting the cables but being careful not to tighten them around Orkahm in the process. When he was done, the Matoran practically fell into his arms.

"What happened?" Matau asked. "Where is the Great Disk?"

"Not here. I wish it was! I wish I could give it away right now, with all the trouble it has caused me," Orkahm said, his voice filled with exhaustion. "Ever since I found it, I've been followed by two beings, one huge, one with four legs, not to mention having Ahkmou on my back about it. Then I got this message."

He handed Matau a small tablet. It read:

The disk you found is vital to the security of the city. Bring it to Moto-Hub sector 3 and take the marked chute.

"But you didn't bring the disk," Matau said.

"I thought it might be a trick. Maybe they wanted to follow me to where it was hidden. No sooner did I get here than these cables snapped tight around me. I heard a voice say that someone would be along soon to talk to me. But no one came until you, Matau."

"You know who I am?" Matau said, surprised.

"Of course! Only you would be foolish enough, reckless enough, to come after me here. You were a danger to everyone on the road as a rider, and you will probably be a danger as a Toa, too. But thank you."

For the first time in his life, Matau found he had nothing to say. It was just as well, too, for if he had spoken he would never have heard the slithering sound coming from among the cables. He shot a look at the web only long enough to see three Morbuzakh vines working their way toward them.

"We have to get out of here!" he shouted.

Now Orkahm saw the vines, too, and was backing away. "How? The chute only goes in one direction, and it's too high up to jump to anyway. We're trapped!"

"Toa-heroes are never trapped," Matau said, doing his best to sound the way he imagined a Toa Metru should. He grabbed Orkahm and yelled, "Hang on!" as the twin aero slicers on his back began to whirl.

It wasn't easy getting off the ground with the extra weight of Orkahm, but they managed it with barely an inch to spare. The vines wrapped themselves around the chute struts and snaked their way after the two, but by now Matau was flying too high and too fast for them to catch.

"How did you know this would work?" Orkahm asked.

"I'm a Toa-hero. This is what we do," Matau answered. He decided it was best to keep to himself the fact that he'd had absolutely no idea whether the stunt would work and just took the chance.

Maybe that is what being a Toa-hero is really about in the end, he thought as he flew over Le-Metru. *Taking the chances you have to take. Doing the things no one else is able to do.*

Matau banked sharply and headed for the center of the metru. *I think I could get to like this,* he said to himself with a smile.

Onewa, Toa of Stone, ran at full speed through the Sculpture Fields of Po-Metru. Unfortunately, full speed was not all that fast. His new body was built for strength, not sprinting.

"I need a Mask of Speed," he muttered to himself. "If a Toa of Stone has to do this sort of thing, he needs whatever help he can get."

He pushed the thought of masks out of his mind. He had no idea what Mask of Power he was wearing, what it might do, or even how to make it work. He hoped that eventually that would change, but for now there was no point in worrying about it. Onewa had a mission to perform, so, legs aching and heartlight flashing rapidly, he kept running.

The Sculpture Fields were home to hundreds of statues, most of them far too big to fit in even the largest Po-Metru warehouse. Onewa's goal was one particular work of art, with a very unique feature: a Matoran named Ahkmou was sitting on top of it.

"Hey, Onewa," the Matoran shouted. "What gets harder to catch the faster you run?"

Onewa glared at him. "My breath! You can do better than that, Ahkmou."

"Well, hurry up and get me down from here!" the Matoran replied. "You can, can't you?"

"Just stay there. I'll get to you."

As he ran, the Toa of Stone thought back to how he had ended up here. His first stop had been Ahkmou's home, but the Matoran wasn't there. Carvings were scattered all over the floor, furniture was thrown about. Onewa worried that Ahkmou had been kidnapped.

A visit to his workplace had turned up no sign of him either. The other carvers said that their coworker had been jumpy lately, especially after he got a visit from two strangers. One had four legs, the other was a giant, and neither looked like he was bringing good news.

Onewa frowned. The description sounded a lot like the hunter Vakama claimed to have seen, although there was no telling who the brute with him might be. Still puzzling over that, he opened Ahkmou's carver desk. Inside, it was a jumble of items. Onewa spotted not only Po-Metru carving tools but equipment from Ta-Metru, maps from Le-Metru, and assorted items from other parts of the city. It wasn't illegal to have any of that, of course, but why would a Po-Metru carver need it?

Then again, maybe it all means nothing, Onewa thought. *The two strangers could have been some new kind of Vahki that Turaga Dume has put in service. The items in his station could be souvenirs of some kind. I mean, what are the chances Ahkmou has a Great Disk and hasn't told everyone he knows about it already? I don't think Vakama had a "vision." I think he was just seeing things.*

There were still questions to answer, though. Onewa had stumbled on a hidden map of the Sculpture Fields on his way here. One spot was marked, and it was the very same spot at which Ahkmou was waiting now. Who wanted him to go there? And why?

Onewa reached the base of the statue. It was a very long way to the top. Taking a deep breath, he dug his two new tools, called proto pitons, into the stone and began to climb.

Ahkmou leaned over the side and watched. Then he said, "So how did you do it? Really?"

"How did I do what?"

"Make yourself look like a Toa."

"I don't just look like a Toa," Onewa snapped. "I am a Toa!"

"Oh," Ahkmou said, so quietly Onewa could barely hear him. "I see. You must be one of the six, then. And you were looking for me? Is that why you came out here?"

Onewa dragged himself a little farther up the side of the statue. "Yes. I came out here be-cause a fire spitter has been standing too close to his forge and told me I should. He said you had a Great Kanoka Disk."

Ahkmou shook his head. "I don't know anything about any disk. I'm a carver."

With one last effort, Onewa pulled himself to the top of the statue. He lay there, panting for a moment, before looking up at the Matoran. "So how did you get up here?"

Ahkmou stood up and backed away a few steps. Suddenly, he seemed nervous. "I — um — I just came up to . . ." The Matoran's eyes went wide. "Nidhiki!"

Onewa turned around just in time to catch a fleeting glimpse of a four-legged creature on the field below, vanishing behind a statue.

"Who is —" he began, looking back at Ahkmou. But the Matoran was gone. Onewa leaned over the side and saw Ahkmou climbing swiftly down on a series of spikes wedged into the statue.

"Hey! Come back here!" the Toa shouted, but Ahkmou was already leaping from statue to statue, heading for the exit from the field.

Onewa gave a growl of frustration and

started after him. He had just begun the climb down when he noticed something carved into the top of the statue. It read PO-METRU CHUTE 445.

All right then, Ahkmou, the Toa of Stone said to himself. *I may not be as fast as you, but now I know where you're going.*

Getting out of the Sculpture Fields would be a great deal harder than getting into them had been, that much Onewa was sure of. The ground between his location and the exit was unstable, thanks to years of tilling the soil to recycle protodermis. Half the statues were sinking, and the other half had already disappeared in the marshy ground. Normally, only hopping from one sculpture to another would make for a safe exit.

Onewa paused halfway down the makeshift ladder and began whirling his proto piton. "Toa don't hop," he said. "Not when they can do this."

As smoothly as if he had been doing it for years, Onewa slung the piton toward another statue. The edge of the sharp tool caught the stone and held. After testing it with a few tugs,

Onewa stepped off the climbing spikes and swung through the air.

He looped in a wide arc around the sculpture, even as he readied his other piton. At the apex of his swing, he tossed the second piton and watched it bite into another sculpture. "Yes!" he bellowed, smiling. "Who needs chutes? This is the way a Toa should travel!"

Ahkmou elbowed his way through the crowd at Chute Station 445. This was the busiest station in all of Po-Metru, linking as it did to all the other districts. Getting through it was a nightmare. Ahkmou knew that was most likely the reason he had been directed here. In this mob, anything could happen, and no one would ever notice.

Well, this is one Matoran who doesn't intend to mysteriously disappear, he thought. *I'm catching the next chute, and then let them try and find me.*

Ahkmou felt only one twinge of regret as he headed for the chute to Ta-Metru. He had hoped to somehow get his hands on the Po-Metru Great Disk before he left. But when Toa

Onewa showed up, running suddenly seemed like a better idea.

"At least I lost that big kolhii-head," he grumbled. Then he cast a quick glance back to make sure Onewa hadn't followed him. "Why anyone would make him a Toa, I can't —"

Still searching the crowd for Onewa, Ahkmou slammed right into a pair of pillars and fell over. He sat up, brushed himself off, and was about to snarl something about idiots putting pillars in the middle of a chute station when he noticed something very disturbing.

They weren't pillars. They were legs.

Toa Metru legs.

Ahkmou looked up into the smiling face of Onewa. "Going somewhere?" the Toa asked.

"Just — just back to work," Ahkmou stammered. "Can't, um, spend all day sitting on statues, you know."

"That's funny," Onewa replied, gesturing to the nearby chute. "I didn't know they had moved your carver's table to Ta-Metru."

The Toa reached down and gently grabbed

Ahkmou, lifting him into the air. "Why don't we try this again? Hello, Ahkmou. Where are you going? Why did someone leave a note for you on top of a sculpture? And where is the Great Disk?"

"I don't know what you're talking about! Put me down!" Ahkmou shouted.

Onewa noticed a Vahki responding to the disturbance. The crowd parted to let the security enforcer through. He considered just bolting with the Matoran, but sudden movement would be sure to provoke a pursuit, and there wasn't time for that.

For his part, Ahkmou had not even noticed the Vahki. His attention was riveted by the sudden appearance of Nidhiki, who was watching the action from a shadowy corner of the station with a sinister grin on his face. The Matoran frantically weighed the choice between an angry Toa or a smiling, four-legged hunter and found it wasn't any choice at all.

"Okay, tell you what," Ahkmou said quickly. "I'll help you find the Great Disk, but we have to go now. Understand? Now!"

Onewa glanced at the Vahki, who was still a short distance away. When he looked over his shoulder to make sure the other direction was clear, he spotted Nidhiki withdrawing into the shadows. The Toa's eyes narrowed at the sight of him.

"Sure, Ahkmou," Onewa said quietly. "I think I do understand."

"One of them is lying."

Vakama's words were hard, but his tone was very soft. The Toa were sitting in the shadow of the Great Temple, sharing the tales of their adventures. When the stories were finished, it didn't take a vision to know something was very wrong.

"What's that you're whisper-saying, firespitter?" asked Matau.

Vakama glanced at the six Matoran, who were standing off to the side and looking uncomfortable. "It's just — look at what happened. We went out looking for six Matoran, and each of them was gone. They were lured away and promised whatever they wanted most in return for a

Great Disk. Meanwhile, we ran into 'accidents' and sabotage every step of the way. Someone didn't want us to find them."

"And you think one of the Matoran betrayed the others?" asked Nuju. "What about that four-legged monster and his friend? Couldn't they be behind all of this?"

Vakama hesitated. Nokama leaned over and said, "Go ahead, Vakama. Tell us."

"I've seen the four-legged one before," Vakama said quietly. "His power and his rage were . . . frightening. I don't think he would bother with such elaborate methods to lure the Matoran. He would have just taken them."

"But which one can it be?" Nokama asked. "They all knew where to find a Great Disk. They all had reasons to dislike one of us. If anything, we have too many clues: notes from Ahkmou to Vhisola, notes from Vhisola to Tehutti, Ta-Metru tools, Le-Metru chute maps. Where do we start?"

"You are looking at what they have in common, Nokama," said Whenua. "When an archivist is trying to solve a mystery of the past, he looks for what is uncommon, out of place. What is different about one of them?"

Nuju frowned. "Old methods won't solve this, historian."

"No, Whenua has a point," said Nokama. "For example, each of the Matoran recognized us as Toa Metru. Someone must have told them we had transformed. But none of them ever referred to six Toa, did they? Each Matoran only seemed to know about the Toa from his or her own metru. So maybe —"

"You're wrong," cut in Onewa. "I didn't mention it before. I didn't think it was important. But when I talked to Ahkmou on top of the sculpture, he said something odd. He said, 'You must be one of the six.' And he seemed to know our four-legged friend. He called him by name — Nidhiki."

All eyes went to the Po-Matoran, who was standing apart from the others. "From what you said, Onewa, Ahkmou was the only one who lied about knowing the location of a Great Disk," said Nuju. "All the others practically bragged about it."

"Ahkmou's name was on the note to Vhisola," said Nokama.

"There was protodermis dust from Po-Metru near the sabotaged vat controls," said Vakama.

"Ahkmou was asking Ehrye about the Great Disks," added Nuju.

"Orkahm said Ahkmou need-wanted his disk very badly," said Matau.

"And Ahkmou knew about Nui-Jaga, enough to use the idea of one to lure Tehutti to the Archives," finished Whenua.

There was a long, uncomfortable silence, finally broken by Nokama. "Do you think . . . ? Why would he do that?"

"I say we ask him," said Onewa, rising. "And then we haul him to the Vahki."

"No!" snapped Vakama. "We mustn't!"

"Fire-spitter, I am getting tired of you giving orders," Onewa growled, taking a step toward the Toa of Fire. "Who made you leader? Maybe it's time we found out just which is more power-ful, fire or stone!"

Nokama stood and placed herself between them. "Stop it! Metru Nui is in danger. This is no time to fight among ourselves!"

"If you had something besides rocks in your head, carver, you would understand," said Whenua. "Even if Ahkmou is the traitor, he is still the only one who knows where the Po-Metru disk is hidden. We need him. But if you feel like you can't keep an eye on him, well, I —"

"Listen, you dusty librarian, I found him, and I can keep him in line!" snapped Onewa. "At least until I have the Great Disk in my hands."

"Our job has just begun," said Nokama. "If Ahkmou has betrayed Metru Nui, he is a danger to us all, and so is that Nidhiki. Maybe they are working together, or maybe not, but we must beware of both."

"Or maybe they need to beware of us," answered Onewa.

"Nokama is right," said Vakama. "We have to find the Great Disks before it's too late. And we have to keep an eye on all the Matoran while we're doing it. The Morbuzakh is not our only enemy."

Their conversation was interrupted by the ugly sound of a protodermis structure snapping in two. They turned to see Morbuzakh vines hauling the broken remains of a small Ga-Metru temple into the sea.

"As if we need more than one, with that thing around," said Onewa. "Let's go. We have disks to find and a really nasty weed to rip out by the roots."

EPILOGUE

Turaga Vakama paused. The memories of his days as a Toa Metru were powerful ones. There were many times he thought he might never get the chance to tell the tales of Metru Nui and the struggle to save it. Now the words spilled from him like a flood, and he found it almost too much to bear. Toa Lhikan . . . the forges of Ta-Metru . . . his life as a Toa . . . all so long ago.

"That can't be the end of the story," said Takanuva, Toa of Light. "I mean, there is more, isn't there?"

Turaga Vakama smiled. "You were the Chronicler before you were a Toa, Takanuva, and that questioning spirit still lives on in you. Always you seek to know what is hidden. But you are right, that is only the beginning of my tale."

"Did you find the Great Disks?" asked Tahu Nuva. "Did you defeat the Morbuzakh? We must know!"

"And so you shall," said Vakama. "But I am weary, and there is much work still to be done. I will continue my tale tomorrow. Before I am done, you will know why we fought so hard for Metru Nui — and why we were forced to leave. Mata Nui, in his wisdom, brought us to this beautiful island that bears his name. But home will always be Metru Nui."

"Very well, then," said Gali, Toa Nuva of Water. "We will leave you for now, wise one. I know I feel the need for a long talk with Turaga Nokama, and I am sure my brothers have similar ideas."

"Indeed," answered Kopaka, Toa Nuva of Ice, quietly. "There have been far too many secrets kept on this island."

The Toa Nuva filed away, heading in different directions. Only Takanuva remained behind with the Turaga of Fire.

"What troubles you, Toa?" asked Vakama. "Was my tale not what you expected?"

"It's not that," said Takanuva. "I have been a Matoran and now I am a Toa, and yet I still do not remember this city of Metru Nui! Why?"

"You will learn all, in time. Perhaps we should have shared all of this with you long ago, but we felt it would be cruel to remind you of a home you might never see again."

Takanuva nodded. "Perhaps that was wise, Turaga. But tell me, when you lived in Metru Nui — was it wonderful?"

"Wonderful . . . and terrible," said the Turaga. "I fear that when I have finished my tale, the Toa will have learned the true meaning of darkness."